My Precious Little Bear

Claire Freedman

Gavin Scott

Cartwheel
B·O·O·K·S ®

SCHOLASTIC INC.
New York Toronto London Auckland
Sydney Mexico City New Delhi Hong Kong

The sun is rising in the sky.
Hooray! Our day's begun.
My mommy smiles. "Let's go and play!"
We're off to have some fun!

My Precious Little Bear

The long grass by the water's edge
is great fun to explore.
I spot some frogs and butterflies
we've never seen before!

The bees are buzzing happily,
and lead us to a treat:
Some sweet and sticky honeycomb
that tastes so good to eat!

We walk among the shady trees
and find a path to follow.
It leads us to a furry friend,
who peeps out from a hollow.

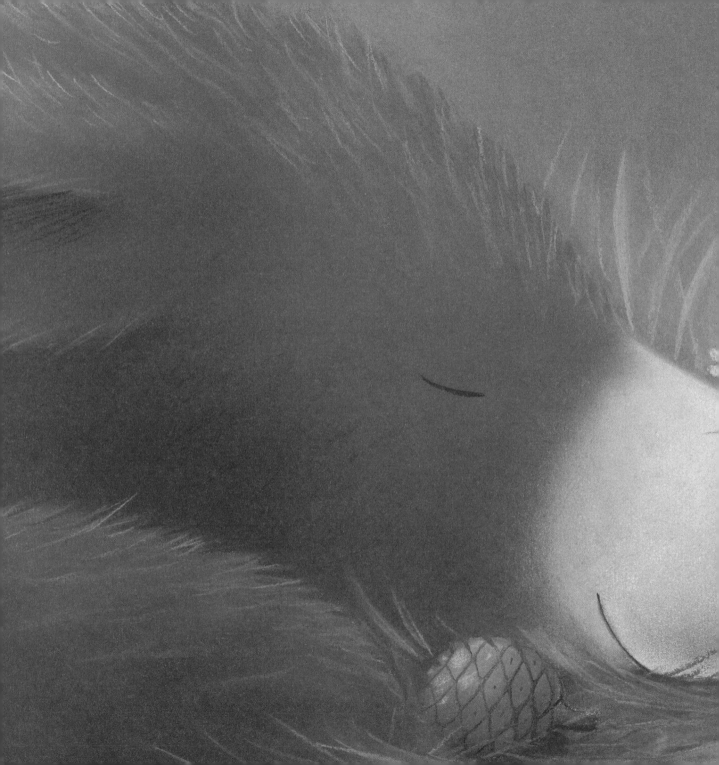

While Mommy stretches out to snooze,
I creep up on tiptoes
and pick a feathery blade of grass
to tickle on her nose!

We race up to the riverbank
and dive into the pool.
I like it when we swim down deep —
the water's icy cool!

I love to watch the shiny fish
that dart and splash and play.
But when I touch one with my paw,
it always slips away!

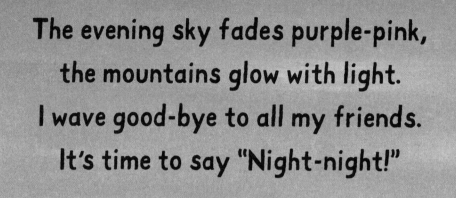

The evening sky fades purple-pink,
the mountains glow with light.
I wave good-bye to all my friends.
It's time to say "Night-night!"

All snuggled warmly in my bed,
I yawn, "I've had such fun!"
"Me too, my little bear," smiles Mom,
"I love you, precious one."

ISBN 978-0-545-44047-9

Text copyright © 2010 by Claire Freedman.
Illustrations copyright © 2010 by Gavin Scott.
All rights reserved. Published by Scholastic Inc. SCHOLASTIC, CARTWHEEL BOOKS, and
associated logos are trademarks and/or registered trademarks of Scholastic Inc.

12 11 10 9 8 7 6 5 4 3 2   12 13 14 15 16 17/0

Printed in the U.S.A.   40

First Scholastic paperback printing, April 2012